A PARTRIDGE in The WE TREE

For my in-laws and favorite houseguests
Charlotte, Beth, Lindsey, Robbie, and Justin;
and my inspiring nieces Aubree and Kamree—AB

PENGUIN WORKSHOP
An imprint of Penguin Random House LLC, New York

First published in the United States of America by Penguin Workshop,
an imprint of Penguin Random House LLC, New York, 2022

Visit us online at penguinrandomhouse.com.

Library of Congress Cataloging-in-Publication Data is available.

Manufactured in China

ISBN 9780593384862 (paperback)   10 9 8 7 6 5 4 3 2 1 TOPL
ISBN 9780593384886 (library binding)   10 9 8 7 6 5 4 3 2 1 TOPL

A Partridge in The WE TREE

ASHLEY BELOTE

Penguin Workshop

Ever since Bear found friendship
among The We Tree, the group
celebrated everything together.

Then Christmas arrived, and everyone's
family came to join in the festivities . . .

On the first day of Christmas,
we welcome festively . . .

SNEEZING
SNOWBEAR

HELLO
My name is:
Partridge

a partridge to
The We Tree.

. . . two
spruced-up cats.

. . . and a partridge
to The We Tree.

BLUE
SPRUCE

That will be fun to clean up . . .

On the third day of Christmas, we welcome festively . . .

... two spruced-up cats, and a partridge to The We Tree.

On the fourth day of Christmas,
we welcome festively ...

. . . four
flocking birds.

SMACK!

Ouch! That's going
to leave a mark . . .
and a smudge . . .

. . . three French squirrels,
two spruced-up cats, and a
partridge to The We Tree.

On the fifth day of Christmas,
we welcome festively . . .

... four flocking birds,
three French squirrels,
two spruced-up cats,
and a partridge to
The We Tree.

On the sixth day of Christmas,
we welcome festively . . .

. . . six mice a-knitting.

. . . five manatees,
four flocking birds,
three French squirrels,
two spruced-up cats,
and a partridge to
The We Tree.

I do NOT look good in hats . . .

On the seventh day of Christmas, we welcome festively . . .

... seven skunks a-skating!

Garland
FOR
BEAR

... six mice a-knitting, five manatees,
four flocking birds, three French squirrels,
two spruced-up cats, and a partridge to The We Tree.

On the eighth day of Christmas, we welcome
festively ...

19

. . . eight goats a-milking.

... seven skunks a-skating, six mice a-knitting,
five manatees, four flocking birds, three French squirrels,
two spruced-up cats, and a partridge to The We Tree.

On the ninth day of Christmas, we welcome festively ...

... nine possums prancing!

Aren't you nocturnal?! Our guest space is getting a little full ...

. . . eight
goats a-milking,
seven skunks
a-skating, six mice
a-knitting, five manatees,
four flocking birds,
three French squirrels,
two spruced-up cats,
and a partridge to
The We Tree.

On the tenth day of
Christmas, we welcome
festively . . .

23

. . . nine possums prancing, eight goats a-milking,
seven skunks a-skating, six mice a-knitting,
five manatees, four flocking birds, three French
squirrels, two spruced-up cats,
and a partridge to
The We Tree.

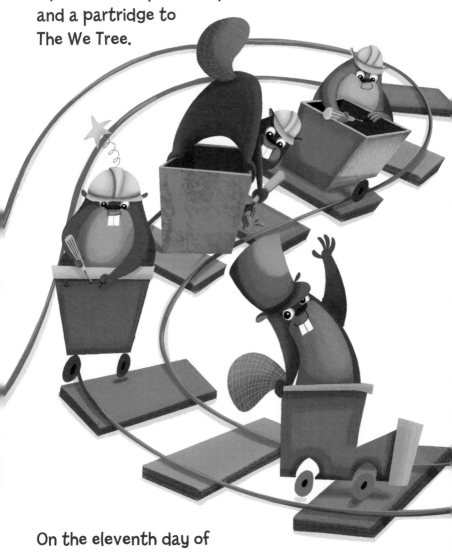

On the eleventh day of
Christmas, we welcome festively . . .

... ten beavers building, nine possums prancing, eight goats a-milking, seven skunks a-skating, six mice a-knitting ...

... five manatees, four flocking birds, three French squirrels, two spruced-up cats, and a partridge to The We Tree.

On the twelfth day of Christmas, we welcome festively ...

. . . twelve brown bears baking.

. . . eleven bees a-buzzing, ten beavers building,
nine possums prancing, eight goats a-milking,
seven skunks a-skating, six mice a-knitting,
five manatees, four flocking birds,
three French squirrels, two spruced-up
cats, and a partridge . . .

Wait . . . where
did he go?

Partridge?
Partridge!
PARTRIDGE!!